SHORT STORIES FOR CURIOUS KIDS

S C Dann

Also available by S. C. Dann

Madder's World

Madder's World Two (part one)

Madder's World Two (part two)

Blitz Spirit & Animal Poems

Mad Old Lady & Poems for children

A Curious First Day & Pirate Poems

Copyright

First published in Great Britain in 2016 with CreateSpace by Samantha Dann.

ISBN-13: 978-1537386300
ISBN-10:1537386301

For Andy and Janice

xxxx

~ CONTENTS ~

'It's the books you read when you're young that stay

with you always.'

– J.K. Rowling

BLITZ SPIRIT

SPIRIT

S C Dann

'A dog's unconditional love can never be measured by its owner's possessions.'

– S.C. Dann

BLITZ SPIRIT

My lungs inhale an acrid smell as I open my eyes to an intense orange glow, shadowed by billowing clouds of black smoke and dust, moving over me like evil spirits. I blink rapidly to wash away the grit in my watery eyes. My body aches as I shift on the hard, jagged rubble jabbing into my ribs.

The nightmare started when Charlie and I heard a deafening, whirring sound. It rose and fell in pitch, like the whine of a toddler, but louder. Charlie stood as still as a statue, staring wide-eyed into the late afternoon sky. His voice quivered when he shouted 'Sirens!' He grabbed our ball and started running towards the park exit. He called my name several times, turning only once to make sure I was close behind.

My heart pounded as I followed my best friend. I follow Charlie everywhere. I can sense when he's happy or sad, and when he's scared. Was Charlie running from the thunder I could hear in the distance? I doubted it – I have much better hearing than Charlie, and I was struggling to hear it over the sirens.

I darted along the pavement as close to Charlie as I could without knocking into his heels, focusing on the backs of his legs streaked with dirt. He was wearing grey shorts, worn black leather shoes with loose laces and grey socks that had slid down his ankles. His shoes tapped rhythmically against the pavement, interrupted only by short pauses when he checked for traffic.

The rumbling grew louder. I was sure that Charlie could hear it now. I began to tremble – I *hate* thunderstorms. But the noise was a continuous hum, not the intermittent rumbles that I'd heard during previous storms.

We darted past the shops – Charlie likes the lady in the sweet shop, and I like the friendly man who owns the butcher's. However, Charlie seemed in no mood to stop and talk to anyone today.

My breathing was laboured as we turned the next corner and headed down a road lined with terraced houses not far from our house near London's Docks. Apart from a few bewildered individuals, staring up at the sky, most people I saw seemed to be running.

The rumbling sounded much louder now. It seemed to be following us like the vengeful bees that'd chased Charlie when he'd poked the hive in his grandad's garden with a stick last summer. His grandad had been *very* cross and lectured Charlie about the importance of bees in the pollination of flowers, telling him that we'd pay a huge price for disturbing such peaceful creatures that live in harmony with their neighbours, *if* left alone.

The humming grew louder still. This time, it seemed that the bees were coming whether Charlie had provoked them or not.

Panting heavily, I looked up. Hundreds of dark bird-like shadows flew over us. It was then that I realised the humming was coming from something larger and more dangerous than angry bees.

Charlie kicked open the gate to our house, frantically calling my name as he gestured for me to follow. But my heart was pumping with primal fear. I felt waves of confused messages pulsating through my nervous system, telling my brain not to follow. I was overwhelmed by an urge to take cover elsewhere. But I couldn't leave Charlie...

Hundreds of whistling objects started falling from the sky. Petrified, I turned in a circle, watching the black birds drop their whistling objects like ripened conkers dropping from a shaken tree.

The world seemed to pause...followed by a moment of terrifying silence. Then, came the explosions.

The huge conkers hit the ground. Shockwaves pulsated through it, lifting and splitting the ground's surface in waves of flying debris. Deafened, my body flew through the air in silence. I saw flashes of bright orange and yellow mixed with rising dust and flying rubble. Then, my world went black.

I don't remember any more until I awoke a moment ago. Struggling to breathe in the thick smoke, I roll over and scramble to my feet. Sharp pains are shooting through one of my legs as I try to gain a stable foothold on the loose rubble, causing several broken bricks to roll away from the heap.

Trembling, I look around. *I can't see Charlie...*My heart begins to flutter with panic as I look through the eye-stinging smoke, billowing from the unrecognisable devastation. *What happened to the houses?* Several no longer have their roofs, and some have lost most of their walls, too. Those remaining point up through the flames like jagged dragon's teeth.

I limp forward on the unstable debris. *Where's Charlie's house?* I feel disorientated. I remember being hurled through the air by the blast before I blacked out. *Which way did I land?* I stumble back several paces – the heat from the blazing houses is too intense. Snatching panicked breaths, I scramble over the rubble, trying to avoid the thickest pockets of smoke and the suffocating heat. *I have to find Charlie!*

The hot air crackles all around me as I continue up and over mounds of debris, searching for anything familiar – something that might lead me to Charlie. As I limp over the next mountain of rubble, I can see dark silhouettes aiming streams of water at the flickering flames. *One of them might be him...*

I move from one person to the next. But each dark figure is too big to be Charlie. I try to communicate with them. I ask each one if they know where I can find my missing pal. Some ignore me and continue fighting the flames, while others at look me with a mixture of bewilderment and pity. However, none of them understands me – Charlie is the only person who ever understands me. *Where are you Charlie?*

My head is aching as I wander from one almost identical pile of rubble to the next, searching for my friend. My tongue feels dry. But I have no time to find water – I have to look for Charlie.

I hear an almighty crash and dart out of the way as a wall from a nearby house comes crashing down, spreading a cascade of rubble. A plume of smoke and orange flames blows towards me. Panting, I turn my head and scuttle away from the intense heat.

Moments later, my heart leaps as the light from the flames illuminates a round brown leather object resting close to a large piece of splintered wood. I stumble on the debris, shifting and sliding under me, as I take each precarious step forward. My eyes widen and my heart pounds in my chest as I move closer. *Could it really be what I think it is?* I move faster, despite the acute pains shooting through my leg. As soon as I touch the object, it rolls away from the piece of wood. *It's Charlie's ball!*

I slide down the rolling rubble towards the football, which appears to have suffered hardly any damage. *How did it manage to survive unscathed when surrounded by such devastation?* I pick it up, being careful to hold it very gently. Charlie usually carries his football because I accidentally punctured his last one. With tears in his eyes, he'd told me off for being too rough and said we wouldn't be able to play with it again because it would go flat once all the air escaped through the hole. He was right: the ball deflated and Charlie's parents had to buy him a new one.

Eyes stinging, I start searching the area where I found the ball. *Charlie must be here somewhere: he was holding the ball when the blast happened.*

Some people run past me dragging long hoses. One man shouts at me while another tries shooing me away from the burning houses. But I'm *not* going anywhere without finding my friend.

I'm holding the ball as gently as I can. When I find Charlie, I want to make him smile. I want to give him his precious ball back undamaged, so that we can forget what's happened and go back to playing football again.

I scan every inch of the rubble. My mouth is dry and my breathing is laboured as I weave through the billowing, black smoke. The heat is zapping what little energy I have left. *Where is he?* Limping, I gaze up at the orange sky...*The whole world seems to be on fire!*

As I watch the flickering sparks from the flames rise and disperse, my senses become alert. Through the overpowering smell of smoke and dust, I sense a hint of something that makes my heart flood with warmth. Sniffing, I shuffle one way: the scent fades. I change direction: the scent is stronger. I continue forward, adjusting my position where necessary. *I'm closer...keep going...*

The smell is so strong now that my aching body begins to quiver with excitement. I circle the spot where the scent is strongest. If I move either side of the spot the smell becomes slightly weaker. I push my nose against the rubble. *The smell's definitely coming from here!*

I look up to find more people have arrived. Some of them have come in vehicles just like the one that took Charlie away when he'd been stung by the bees. *Charlie told me these people helped him...I wonder if they'll help me now?*

I begin to paw at the rubble, pushing it away from the spot under my feet. I pant heavily. My body feels weary, and my painful leg refuses to do all I ask. But if I continue digging, someone might realise what I'm doing and help. Two people scurry past. But they ignore me. *Will no one help?* I dig and dig. Dust from the rubble makes me sneeze. Through blurred vision, I continue to move the debris. *If I have to, I'll do this all by myself – I won't give up!* The scent becomes stronger.

I can hear myself whimpering with anguish and frustration. But I don't care if the whole world hears me – the most important thing in my life could be centimetres from me now! A surge of inner strength is released, forcing me to forget my increasing pain and concentrate solely on digging.

I can hear voices gathering around me. 'What's he doing? What have you found, boy?' But I'm so engrossed in digging that I don't turn round. 'There must be something under there!' says another voice.

I can't stop. I keep digging. The scent is *really* strong now.

My collar tightens around my neck. 'Come back, boy!' says a deep voice. But I'm strong, and I manage to resist. *I have to keep digging!* They pull again – harder this time. *Leave me alone...I have to keep digging!* The collar tightens round my neck, making me writhe. I snatch short panicked breaths from the smoky air. *Leave me alone!*

'Let me take him,' says another panicked voice.

I recognise this person's voice, even though it's quivering with fear. I instantly snap out of my trance-like state and stop digging. I look behind me and see Mum's tearful face as she grabs my collar and pulls me back. Consumed with relief, I whiz round and bound into her, barking wildly, ignoring the excruciating pain in my leg.

Then, I dart towards Dad as he runs past. 'Good boy, Jack, I think you've found Charlie!' he says, patting my head before dropping on to his knees next to the shallow hole I've made in the rubble.

'Woof! Woof!' *They've come to help!* 'Woof! Woof!'

'Everyone, move the rubble from this end first!' said the person with the deep voice who seemed to be taking charge. 'We need to make sure he has enough air.'

Air! Charlie's losing air? I let out an involuntary whine – Charlie had had to throw his punctured ball away when there wasn't enough air inside.

Mum knelt beside me, patting my back harder than she probably realised. Sobbing, she said, 'It's okay, Jack, he'll be okay – he'll be out in no time.'

I release another involuntary whine. If Mum and Dad had to buy another ball...would they have to buy another Charlie? *I don't want another Charlie!*

My heart pounds as I stare, unblinking, at Dad and the rest of the helpers removing handfuls of rubble from the spot where I'd been digging. I'm trembling. Jabbing pains are passing through my leg. I feel as if I'm going to collapse. But I need to be strong. I have to give Charlie his ball when he comes out. *The ball!* I scan my surroundings and stagger forward, dragging Mum with me.

Luckily, the ball's still intact and where I left it. While Mum is cursing me for almost wrenching her arm off, I carefully pick the ball up. *I must be careful – I must make sure I don't puncture it.*

'Oh, Jack' – Mum pauses to sob, tears streaming down her face – 'we can't play ball now.'

As soon as we turn round, Mum lets go of my collar and stumbles towards the disturbed rubble.

Free to investigate, I limp around the group of helpers, looking through the gaps between them as they bend down to lift something from the debris. *What's happening?*

Mum lets out a muffled scream: her hand is pressed over her mouth.

'Lift the door on three!' said the person with a deep voice. 'One...two...three!'

A few of the helpers move a severely damaged door while the rest reach into the hole. 'He's lucky this was covering him,' says one of the people discarding the door. Another adds, 'At least he's had some air under there.'

My heart is racing. *Charlie still has some air!* I sit with the ball between my teeth. *I'm a good boy. When Charlie comes out, he'll see that I've looked after his ball for him.*

A dusty black shoe falls to the ground and rolls towards me as they lift a small limp body from the hole in the rubble. *He's covered in dust and dirt. It doesn't look much like Charlie, but it definitely smells like him.* I'm trying to stay still...I'm trying to be good. But I edge forward with the ball in my mouth. My tail is wagging frantically, brushing the debris.

'My son!' cries Mum, taking his tiny limp hand in hers.

I edge forward again. *Look, Charlie, I've kept your ball safe.* My head moves in an arc as he is carried over me and put on a stretcher. I let out a deep guttural whine. *Charlie! I'm here! We can play football again!*

I find a gap between the people gathering around Charlie and push my way through. But Charlie can't see me because his eyes are closed. *Wake up, Charlie! Wake up!* I stare at his dusty face in bewilderment before I finally give up and collapse beside him. The ball that I'd looked after so carefully falls from my mouth and rolls over Charlie's body on to the rubble. I rest my head on his tummy – he feels nice and warm. I'm so tired. I half close my heavy eyelids. *Good idea...I'll shut my eyes too...we'll go to sleep together...*

I peel my eyes open. *How long have I been asleep?* Through misted vision I can see the leather football. *It's safe and still perfectly round.* Someone strokes my head and softly calls my name. My heart flutters with recognition...

Charlie leaps up, turns and darts out of the room. 'Mum! Dad! Look! Jack is waking up!'

I know this house – it's Charlie's grandad's house. I try to jump up. I want to bounce around and greet everyone like usual. But I can't move my leg. Charlie charges back into the room. He drops to his knees beside me, grabs me in his arms and nuzzles into my neck. Despite my dry mouth, I lick and lick and lick his face. *Charlie is awake! We can play football now!*

My body aches as I try to lift myself from the floor again. Mum and Dad both hurry into the room, beaming.

Mum bends down and says softly, 'Stay there, boy, you've broken your leg. Don't worry, you'll be running around again in a few weeks' time.'

Dad pushes my water bowl towards me. 'You deserve a lot more than water for saving our son. But I'm sure Mother will be treating our war hero to the best cuts of meat she can get her hands on for the rest of your days – you can count on that.' He pats my head and smiles.

Charlie hugs me tighter. 'You're the best dog in the world, Jack! I knew you'd never give up!'

Dad lifts the bowl nearer to my mouth. As I move my head to drink, I focus on Charlie's ball. *I can't wait to play football again!* I lap up the water eagerly, flicking droplets over everyone. *I'll be fit and ready again in no time – you'll see!*

Charlie laughs. 'You messy dog!'

Grandad totters in from the kitchen and chuckles. 'Now that's what I call true "Blitz Spirit"!'

MAD OLD LADY

S C Dann

'People generally see what they look for and hear what they listen for.'

– Harper Lee

MAD OLD LADY

I slam the door behind me. Biting my bottom lip, I charge down the path, yanking my school rucksack onto my back. The curtain twitches as I walk past the window. *I don't care what she says – I'm not going! If Mum wants me to go, she'll have to drag me there herself!* I purse my lips and raise my chin as I charge forward through the spitting rain.

I kick a stone into a puddle. *I know it was wrong to call our neighbour a 'crazy old battleaxe'...but she is bonkers! Everyone says she's as mad as a bucket-full-of-frogs!* I release an exasperated groan. *Mum's overreacting – all this aggravation because I failed one stupid biology test!*

'Hi Stacey! What's up?'

My head whips round. 'Nothing.' I turn away from Cameron's concerned blue eyes and look back at the rain streaming through the cracks in the pavement, which remind me of my fractured relationship with Mum.

'Slow down!' he urges. His tall, slim frame stoops a little as he jogs beside me. 'Your face is scrunched up like you're chewing on a wasp and you expect me to believe there's *nothing* wrong!' Cameron squeezes his hands into his damp trouser pockets.

I take a deep breath. 'It's my *mother* again! I can't seem to do *anything* right!' I shove a long, wayward strand of hair back into the hood of my jacket – it's raining heavier now.

Cameron's dark, saturated hair is sticking to his forehead. He pushes his fingers through the thick roots to restore his usual slick quiff. 'What's she moaning at you about now?'

'I called Mrs Craven a "crazy old battleaxe".' I tighten my lips in anger as Cameron almost falls over laughing. 'What's so funny?'

Cameron sucks in his cheeks to stem his laughter, hugging his tummy as he continues to jog beside me.

I inhale deeply. 'You wouldn't be laughing if *your* mother said you'd have to go to Mrs Craven's house – *would you?*' I grit my teeth, visualising my mother's face in every puddle as I stomp through them, making her features disintegrate with each splash. *It was a really bad idea to wear shoes instead of boots for school today.*

Cameron's smile slowly disappears. 'Your mum *can't* send you to Mrs Craven's house!'

I stop walking and look up, rain driving into my face. 'Exactly!' I exclaim. 'What am I going to do?'

Cameron appears to be staring at nothing as he says, 'The old woman's always digging huge holes in her garden...it's where she *buries* children who dare to go *anywhere* near her house.' He pushes his fingers through his wet hair again, holding them there for a few seconds before moving them. The rainwater trickles down his back, making him shiver.

My eyes narrow. 'That's *not* making me feel any better!' I release a deep guttural groan.

Cameron continues, 'She blacks-out her windows so she can perform evil spells... look into her unblinking eyes and you'll turn to stone...hidden under her long dress she's supposed to have more than two legs–'

He jolts sideways as Tom runs into him. 'All right, mate?' asks Tom, breathlessly. 'You two are late for school today.'

Cameron pushes Tom away. 'And you're *early* I suppose?'

'Early for me' – Tom grins, showing the braces covering his teeth – 'I'm late every day, but if I walk in with you two it'll make me look earlier than usual.'

I start walking again. 'I bet we get a detention for being late and you don't...How do you get away with it?'

'It's all about the preparation,' he puffs as he increases his pace to keep up, but he's overweight, so his breathing is laboured.

'What preparation?' asks Cameron, rolling his eyes at me.

Tom sneezes and then wipes his nose on the sleeve of his blazer – he hasn't had the sense to bring a coat. 'It starts with a rumour.'

'I'm in the middle of a major life crisis' – I glare at him – 'and you want to talk about spreading *stupid* rumours.'

Tom blurts, 'Well, if you *don't* want to actually tell a lie, but you *do* want a story exaggerated for your own benefit, then it helps to "accidentally" release a snippet of the news first. Then, before you can blink, the leaked information is blown up as it's passed from one gossip to the next.'

Cameron and I just look blankly at Tom's dripping-wet face as he pants, jogging along beside us.

Tom groans before explaining, 'If I tell Blabbermouth Benny that I'm nervous about going to the hairdressers tonight, by the time Dippy Davina hears the story my own mother would probably be accused of planning to saw my head off!' His eyes widen as he looks from me to Cameron. He lifts both arms before dropping them to his sides. 'Recently I "accidentally" told Blabbermouth that my mum had been sick. By the time the news had travelled around the school, half the kids and most of the teachers were smothering me with sympathy. Using different voices, he mimics, '"How are things at home, Tom? Is it true that your mother can't work because she's really ill? When does your mother come out of hospital? How long has she got to live?" It's why I don't get a detention for being late – they all feel sorry for me.'

'But' – Cameron pauses – 'your mum's *not ill*... she's pregnant. That's why she's puking up.'

'You've lied to everyone.' I interject.

We rush through the school gates. The grumpy biology teacher – Mr Drayton – is standing by the hedge under a huge umbrella, waiting to write down the names of any latecomers.

Tom taps the side of his nose. 'No...that's my point...*I* haven't *lied* to *anyone*...' He darts left, heading for his form class. 'Morning, Mr Drayton.'

'Morning, Tom,' replies the teacher. He clears his gritty throat as he swings round and shouts, 'No running in the school grounds!' He shudders as his gangly frame retreats back under his umbrella.

Tom turns and shouts, 'Yes, Sir!' Then, he disappears through the double doors leading to the new block.

Head down, I hurry past Mr Drayton.

'And where do you two think you are going?' he asks in his monotone voice. 'Names?'

'Cameron Blake, Sir.'

I sigh. 'Stacey Smyth, Sir.' *Why is he asking for our names when he already knows them?* I stare at him as he struggles to hold the umbrella, the clipboard and the pen. Even though I'm already drenched, I find standing here waiting for him to scribble down our names in the pouring rain particularly irritating when all he has to do is remember them!

Mr Drayton looks up from his spidery writing. 'I'll see you both for a lunchtime detention in room four today – *don't* be late!' He points to the office door. 'Report to the office before you go to your form classes.'

My eyes widen in dismay as I head off with Cameron following close behind. *I do know where the office is!*

'Tom got away with detention *again*,' whispers Cameron.

'By lying,' I add.

'But he hasn't actually–'

'I know he hasn't *actually* lied.' I sigh. 'But he's avoided being totally truthful by not correcting the rumours. No good will come of it – if he's found out, no one will ever believe anything he says again!' I push open the office door. Dripping water all over the corridor, I ring the bell to get the office lady's attention. 'We're late. Mr Drayton told us to come here and report to you.'

Mrs Bell looks at us through the glass divider, pursing her lips. 'Okay...go through before you turn the corridor into a swimming pool.' She unlocks the door and lets us pass into the inner corridor that leads to our lockers.

'See you in Drayton's room at one o'clock,' says Cameron as he heads towards his locker.

I take off my dripping jacket and stuff it into my locker – the fleece lining will take forever to dry out. After forcing the door shut, I lock it and head for my form class, following the mass of overlapping muddy footprints left by the earlier pupils. My feet are squelching in my shoes as I walk past Tom's form class. He waves. I nod back. Even if I wanted to wave, which I don't, my fingers are busy teasing out the knots in my saturated hair. *Straightening my hair this morning had been a complete waste of time. I wish I could start this day all over again. I wish I hadn't called Mrs Craven a 'mad old battleaxe' – even if the old woman is nuts – then I wouldn't have had an argument with Mum, and then I wouldn't be late or have a stupid lunchtime detention with the* *biology teacher! Life can be so...*I open the door to my form class. Everyone turns round.

'You're late!' exclaims Miss Parker. 'Sit down!'

State the obvious, why don't you! Glaring at anyone who is brave enough to make eye contact with me, I sit down and slump over my desk. *I hate Monday mornings, I hate school, I hate biology, I hate Mr Drayton but most of all I hate my mum!*

After suffering another morning of mind-numbing boredom, I head off to room four, biting chunks out of my sandwich – I'm starving after leaving the house without having breakfast. I over-chew each mouthful into an unsavoury pulp, which is as hard to swallow as this 'wonderful' day.

I dash down the corridor and turn into the next, stuffing the rest of my sandwich back in my lunchbox. As I near Mr Drayton's room, I can see Cameron through the glass door panel. *As predicted – there's no sign of Tom in detention.* I run my fingers through my 'gorgeous' hair one last time before I push the door open and slam it shut behind me. Giving Mr Drayton a cursory smile, I weave through the tables to sit next to Cameron who is trying to hide his amusement at my dramatic entrance.

Mr Drayton taps his foot while looking at his watch. 'You're two minutes late, Stacey Smyth.'

I'm sure his boring voice could be used as a method of torture – speak now or we'll make you listen to Mr Drayton! I take a deep breath before saying, 'Your watch might be two minutes fast, Sir.'

The teacher's lips narrow as a rising flush of colour reaches his cheeks. 'You're in no position to act clever around me after your recent test results, Miss Smyth!' He slides his fingers over his trimmed beard, from his cheeks to his chin.

Cameron lowers his head and makes a thumbs-down sign to me under the desk. I look away from Cameron and turn back to Mr Drayton, giving him my most pleasant smile. 'Sorry, Sir.'

'You will be,' snaps the teacher. 'Your mother phoned the school this morning.' He pauses, watching my face change from a smug expression to an oh-no-what-has-she-told-them look! 'She has arranged some extra biology tuition for you after school.'

I let out an exasperated sigh, words screaming in my head: *Muuuuum! I don't believe it – she's already been to see crazy Mrs Craven? My life is becoming a complete –*

Mr Drayton continues, 'And, in addition, you'll be happy to know that I've agreed to give you extra tuition at school – you'll meet me here every lunchtime for a week, and then retake your test at the end.'

My insides feel like water boiling inside a kettle, gradually bubbling until a rush of steam builds behind my burning tear ducts. *I'm not going to cry...*

Cameron's fingers tighten around his pen. 'Great...' he mutters. He shifts in his chair, exchanging a look that tells me I'm doomed.

Mr Drayton interjects, 'Well, Cameron, if you think it's such a "great" idea, maybe you should join her – after all, your test results weren't exactly "great" either, were they?'

Cameron jolts upright, mouth open. But no words leave his lips.

Mr Drayton raises his eyebrows. 'No Buts...Both of you are in detention for a week.' He lobs two biology textbooks in our direction 'Turn to page nine...pollination.'

*My mind feels as if it's about to explode! Biology! Biology! And more biology! If I see another science textbook, I'll scream...*I open my locker and the smell from my damp jacket hits me in the face like the stench of sweaty socks emanating from the boys' locker room. I shove my bag containing the rest of my uneaten lunch inside and pull out my PE kit. *Hockey in the rain...I can't wait!*

Seconds later, a thunderous roar of wet pupils spills into the corridor like a flash flood, signalling the end of lunch.

'Did you enjoy your detention, Stacey?'

I whip round and glower at Tom who is pointing at me and laughing. *He'd better keep a safe distance from me!* He backs away, panting. I shout, 'You think you're *so* clever! I look forward to the day when everyone finds out...' I continue the next part of the sentence in my head...*that you're a liar! Maybe I ought to remind Mr Drayton that Tom also failed his biology test last week.*

I feel no relief when the bell rings at the end of the school day: I'm starving, my damp jacket weighs a tonne, it's *still* raining, my brain's painfully swollen with useless biology facts and now I have to go home and listen to my mum droning on about Crazy Craven. *I hate my life!*

'Stacey!'

I turn round, rain driving into my face, to see Cameron running to catch up. I stop, shoulders hunched, to wait for him. 'I'm warning you, I'm in a *really bad* mood.'

'Drayton's detention wasn't that bad...was it?'

I trudge forward, releasing a guttural groan. 'It's got nothing to do with *that*! What am I going to do about my mum and the mad old lady? Mum told Drayton she'd already made the arrangements.'

Cameron pauses, chewing on his bottom lip. Pushing both hands through his hair he says, 'Why don't I go with you...to Mrs Craven's house...that's if you want me to go?'

I stop dead and stare into his eyes, watching the rainwater drip off the end of his nose. 'Very funny...' *Is he being serious?*

'I mean it...I'll go with you.'

My eyes widen. 'You will?'

'If your mum's already arranged it, why don't we get it over and done with and go straight to Craven's house now?' He smiles. 'If we arrive before she's expecting you, the crazy old lady might be...you know...unprepared...'

I stare at him, confused.

Cameron hesitates, looking for the right words. 'Crazy Craven won't be ready for your visit, so we'll have the upper hand.'

I gulp. 'I'm not sure...' Chewing my thumbnail, I begin to pace forward.

'I'll...keep an eye on you.' He catches me up.

I look him up and down. 'I don't need you to protect me!' Secretly, I'm relieved he's offered to help. I pull my hood forward. *I might feel less...nervous if I'm not on my own.*

'Who are you *protecting* Stacey from?' asks Tom, sniggering. He hurries past, knocking into Cameron's arm.

Cameron grabs Tom's saturated blazer and pulls him back. Tom makes a choking sound as his podgy legs stagger in and out of a puddle.

Dragging Tom with him, Cameron turns to me and says, 'Look, Stacey, another *"willing"* helper.' He glares at Tom and hisses, 'I've had enough of you teasing me all day about Drayton's detention! You're nothing but a lying–'

'Let go!' curses Tom, falling over his own feet as he tries to keep up with Cameron. He wriggles free and straightens his clothes. Mouth open and eyes watering, he pauses before sneezing.

I stop walking and grimace as Tom proceeds to wipe his nose on his sleeve. 'I don't want *him* coming with us!'

'Coming with you where?' asks Tom.

'To Mrs Craven's house,' says Cameron.

Tom gasps. 'You're *mental*! I'm – I'm not going with you to that *mad* woman's house!'

I let out an exasperated groan as I trudge forward, leaving the boys behind. *Great! I've got two of them tagging along now!*

Tom begins to beg, 'Cameron, no, please don't drag me to *Crazy Craven's* house! I'm *starving* – I need my tea! I promise not to laugh at you when you have detention again!'

I hear their footsteps splashing through the puddles behind me – the irregular steps are probably those of Tom, as Cameron pulls him along.

Cameron remains silent as Tom pleads, 'I *promise* not to lie again! I'll tell the truth about my mum not being ill...I'd rather join you in detention than go to that *crazy* woman's house!'

'Too late,' says Cameron. 'If I'm going, then you're going.'

Tom's breathing quickens. 'But...but...she's got four legs and eyes that'll turn you to stone with one look! She'll put an evil spell on all of us!'

The footsteps behind me stop. I turn towards the driving rain, which stings my face. Cameron has let go of Tom and is staring at me, shoulders hunched with his hands in his pockets. Tom is shifting his

42

weight from one foot to the other, looking at the ground. *Cameron's changed his mind...They're both waiting for a get-out-jail-free card.* 'Fine' – I place my hands on my hips – 'if you two are *too scared*, I'll go *all – by – myself!*' I whip round cursing, 'I don't need your help anyway!' I straighten my posture and march forward. *It's not as if I asked for their stupid help!*

I hear them whispering behind me and smile inwardly when their footsteps follow me to Crazy Craven's house.

My heart begins to flutter as I spot the dilapidated house at the end of Crow's Close. Through the diagonal streaks of rain, I see Mrs Craven's uncut hedge, brambles sprouting from it like huge prickly spiders' legs. My fists clench in my pockets as I move closer. I look back at Cameron and Tom who aren't far behind.

I stare at the rickety wooden gate – forming a gap in the hedge – which hangs lopsided by a loop of knotted rope hooked over an ivy-strangled post.

'Coming here is a stupid idea,' whispers Tom, as they move closer.

Cameron whispers back, 'We can't leave Stacey to go in alone...'

I take a deep breath and grit my teeth before saying, 'If you two are too *scared* to come in with me, then go home.'

'No...we're fine, aren't we, Tom?' The pitch of Cameron's voice rose.

'Yeah,' replies Tom. 'I can't *wait* to go in.'

It's so obvious...they're both more frightened than me. Biting my lip, I grab the damp rope and lift it off the gatepost. I jump back as the gate drops and thuds against the stony path – the bottom hinge has rusted away. My heart rate quickens. *I'm not scared...* I clench my fists...*it's only a gate.* Sweat snakes down my spine, making me shiver. Taking deep breaths, I attempt to control my erratic breathing as Cameron leans forward and lifts the wooden gate out of the way. He grimaces as he realises his fingers are smeared with wet, green slime from the gate's moss-covered struts.

Tom begins to edge backwards, the braces on his teeth glinting as he gives us an I'm-getting-out-of-here-now grin. But Cameron's too quick for him. He grabs Tom's wet blazer and drags him with us down Craven's slimy, cobbled path.

None of us speak as we move together in slow synchronized steps. Eyes wide, I scan the lifeless shrubs on either side of the slippery path, which are intertwined with the brambles hanging from the hedge, almost as if it's being pulled towards the house to deliberately block out the light.

My mouth's dry and my heart's pounding as I continue forward. The house is an ugly, small, single-storey dwelling with a tatty oak door set between identical windows positioned on either side. The glass is filthy and the peeled paintwork is so weathered that only traces of the original white paint remain. My eyes dart over the exterior, which is almost entirely enveloped by dark parasitic ivy.

I stop at the front door and take a deep breath...*I'm seriously freaked out...I can't go in there!* The boys are both staring wide-eyed at me as I turn to face them.

Seconds later, Cameron's eyes bulge from their sockets. He shuffles backwards, closely followed by

Tom. *Are they going to leave me here...on my own?* I gulp.

'Stacey, *ruuuuun!*' shouts Tom.

Someone grabs my arm. My body goes rigid. I'm unable to look back as I'm pulled through the door, knocking my shoulder into its frame. I reach out to Cameron, but he's running down the cobbled path as the door slams shut and I'm plunged into darkness.

My panicked breaths seem to fill the poorly lit room as I stagger backwards in a dizzy haze. My elbow knocks against a hard object, which wobbles before crashing to the floor. I whip round. 'Who's there?' My tongue sticks to the roof of my mouth as I swallow. Sharp pains shoot through my elbow as I shuffle one way, then the other, scanning the musty room. I hear someone mumbling – it sounds like a *curse!* 'Ahhhhh!' I scream.

My eyes begin adjusting to the dimly lit room. I see the door and rush back towards it. I yank the handle up and down, pushing my body against it. But it's locked. 'Cameron! Tom! Help *meeeee!*'

I fall against the door trembling and squeeze my eyes shut. *I mustn't look at her...* My laboured breaths sound as if they're coming from a captured beast instead of my own rasping lungs. *She's going to turn me into stone!*

Thud! Thud!

She's moving towards me! I grab the door handle again. The cold metal digs into my palm as I tug it up and down. I pound the rough wooden door with my fist. 'Cameron! *Heeeeelp!*'

Thud! Thud! Thud! Thud!

My heart leaps like a startled deer trapped under my ribcage, sending pulses of fear coursing through my veins. *She's going to kill meeeee!* Tears moisten my eyelashes as I squeeze my closed eyes tighter together.

Click...

A red hue of light penetrates my eyelids. I gasp, inhaling a sharp, quivering gulp of air, and hold my breath. Digging my fingernails into the wooden door, I listen to the nearby shuffles and grunts from someone in the room. *Is it Mrs Craven?*

'I wouldn't have had you here,' echoes a croaky voice, 'if I'd been told you're such a *clumsy oaf!'* She grunts before mumbling, 'Coming here earlier than planned and knocking into *my* furniture...I've had that pot table for years...it was my mother's.'

A hard object pokes me in the chest. My eyes ping open, forcing me to release my held breath. Filling my lungs with sharp panicked gasps, I hold my hands up to cover my eyes. '*Please,* don't turn me into stone...' I jolt backwards as Mrs Craven pokes me in the chest again, harder this time.

'Believe all that *rubbish*...do you?' She tuts. 'You're even more stupid than your mother's led me to believe.' She pauses before saying, 'The "Mad Old Lady's" not turning anyone into stone today, dear.' She removes the thing poking into my chest.

Thud! Thud! Thud! Thud!

I lower my hands and watch Mrs Craven turn her hunched body and waddle towards her fallen pot table, aided by her two walking sticks, thudding against the wooden floorboards. *Those walking sticks make her look like she has four legs...maybe that's why –?*

She lifts leg three and points it at the table. 'Well, pick it up, girl!'

My pulse races as I shuffle forward and reach for one of the table's legs. I slide it closer to me before standing it upright beside a dusty pine table with four mismatched chairs. I stare at the room, wondering how anyone can live in such a poorly decorated, sparsely furnished room. Then, I realise Mrs Craven is glaring at me with her dark, narrowed eyes. I try to turn the grimace on my face into a friendly smile, but her appearance is equally unsettling. She's a scruffy-looking, short, skinny lady with curly, white hair and deathly-pale, wrinkly skin. *It's no wonder people find her creepy. I'm sure a corpse looks more alive.*

'Mmmmm.' She frowns at me. 'Take off that wet coat and follow me...and try not to knock into *anything else.*'

'I'm...sorry...' I mumble, removing my coat and placing it over one of the chairs. I tuck my damp hair behind my ears.

Mrs Craven grunts as she heads towards an internal door.

Thud! Thud! Thud! Thud!

'Erm...Mrs Craven, my friends are waiting outside...'

Mrs Craven stops. Her baggy, grey cardigan flutters away from her flowery dress like a pair of wings as she whips round and points leg four at me. '*I* never invited *them* here' – she waves the walking stick dismissively at the front door before turning back round – '*they* can stay outside.'

Mrs Craven prods the door leading to the next room with one of her sticks. I squint as a rectangle of light floods through, highlighting the old lady's silhouette like an angel. Seconds later, I inhale a waft of intoxicating scent and am spellbound, as if invisible fairies have drifted up my nose and sprinkled fairy dust. Feeling slightly dizzy, I follow Mrs Craven as she totters into the next room.

My eyes begin dancing in their sockets. My vision is dazzled by an array of colours: red, yellow, pink, orange, purple...

Mrs Craven turns and smiles, revealing her crooked teeth. 'Beautiful, aren't they?'

Speechless, I nod.

'My flowers are the most precious things in the world to me,' she continues. 'This one's called Amaryllis.' She lifts her walking stick to point at a stunning red flower. 'I've never been blessed with children, so I nurture my plants and encourage them to grow perfect blooms.' She totters forward and touches the damp petals of a pink rose. 'This one's called Rosa' – she leans over it and inhales – 'she smells gorgeous...have a sniff.'

I shuffle closer. Mrs Craven tilts the ruffled petals towards me. My nose tingles with delight at the wonderful smell, which is mingled with the scent of so many others being blown around the room by a large fan.

Mrs Craven continues to hobble from one flower to the next, sniffing each one and encouraging me to do the same. The damp, warm room is crammed with tables and shelves filled with pots of all sizes. Each one contains a different variety of flowering plant. As we weave around the tables, she tells me their names, whether they are scented and how long they are usually in bloom. She explains how the fan helps to circulate the air, preventing the growth of fungi and garden pests.

The old lady's enthusiasm is infectious. I can't help it...for the first time in my life I'm interested in *biology?* Mrs Craven continues, smiling as she informs me how she tricks the plants into believing it's summer all year round, by increasing the temperature of the room and using special grow lights: artificial electric lights designed to stimulate growth and photosynthesis. I realise now why all the windows in the room are blacked out with crude pieces of card stuck over each pane of glass. *It has nothing to do with her performing evil spells...*

Mrs Craven cackles before saying, 'It's not easy trying to fool my beautiful plants...it's much easier to fool humans. Some people are so *stupid*, they'll believe almost *anything* you tell them.' Her head turns slowly to look up at me. 'Do *you* believe everything you're told?' – her glassy, grey eyes examine me – 'or are *you* brave enough to find out the truth for yourself?'

I turn away, feeling ashamed. *She's aware of all the things people say about her...and she knows I believe them, too...but I'm beginning to wonder if any of the rumours are true.* I clear my throat and point at the first plant I see and ask, 'What's this one called?'

Why did I pick this plant? It's probably the only ugly, flowerless plant in the whole room!

Mrs Craven smiles. 'That's Sarracenia Flava – a carnivorous fly-killing plant. Once attracted by the plant's nectar, the insects fall down its tall stems where they are digested.' She pauses before saying, 'Even plants can lie to fool the brainless.'

Mrs Craven thinks I'm a fool! This makes me determined to prove her wrong. *I'll decide for myself if she's as mad as everyone says, and I'll pass my biology test!* I start bombarding her with questions. Enthused by my rising interest, she talks to me about photosynthesis and pollination. She rests her walking sticks against the wall and shows me how to cross-pollinate the flowers by hand, collecting the pollen from the stamen of one flower using cotton swabs, which she transfers to the stigma of another flower.

As Mrs Craven shuffles to the next table, she leaves her sticks behind. I'm distracted by the sudden change in her posture; she appears to be standing straighter. She flaps a section of card away from the window to point at her garden. 'My garden's a mess. It's full of big holes....'

My eyes widen as I think of the children Cameron says she's buried alive out there. I take a tentative step back. *Am I her next victim? No! She'd never...*

Mrs Craven continues, 'I dig up the soil to fill my pots.' She bends the card back over the window. A smile creeps over her face as she whispers, 'The biggest holes are great for catching prowlers...they've caught a number of naughty kids sneaking into my garden. They fall into the holes, you see.'

I gulp. 'Where...are they now?'

'How would I know!' exclaims Mrs Craven, tottering away from the window. 'Gone!' As long as they never come back to interfere with my plants, I *don't care*...I never invited any of them here!' She whips round and says, 'Go and take a look...if *you* think the children are *still* trapped out there.'

I look straight in her eyes. 'No need, I believe you.' My heart flutters. Secretly, I'm hoping that Cameron and Tom haven't fallen down any holes.

Mrs Craven smiles. 'Follow me. I've a lot to teach you before I go.'

Before she goes? Where's she going? I thought.

I stare at Mrs Craven as she moves towards another door. Unaided by her walking sticks she passes into a smaller room. I blink rapidly as her outline appears to flicker and fade. I rub my eyes. *It must be the change in light...*

'This is where I grow my cuttings, dear,' informs Mrs Craven.

I enter the room to find trays of tiny plants, positioned in neat rows on two large tables, like an army of little green soldiers standing to attention. Mrs Craven's face glows like a mother admiring her children.

I listen as the old lady continues to impart her knowledge with increasing enthusiasm. She shows me how to make a cutting by snipping off a section of stem, removing the lower leaves and placing it into rooting hormone powder. She explains the importance of planting them in potting soil. I watch her nimble fingers gently pressing the cutting into a separate pot. *Mrs Craven's not mad; she's passionate...about plants. She'd do anything to protect them. I wish I'd visited her before today...Then, I wouldn't have failed the biology test.*

Halfway through telling me about the importance of watering each cutting, Mrs Craven stops talking about her plants and says, 'Time to go, dear.'

'What...right now?' I ask.

'Yes, dear,' she says, shooing me back with outstretched arms. 'It's time to go...I must be on my way. Stuff to do, places to go...'

'But...' The intoxicating scent hits me as I step backwards into the room filled with flowers. 'Can – can I come back...tomorrow?' I grab her walking sticks as she hobbles past them.

'Send my love to your mother,' says Mrs Craven, ignoring my question, 'She's a good woman.' She shuffles through to the first room, grabs my coat and passes it to me.

I blink rapidly as my eyes adjust to the dim light. 'Mrs Craven?' For a second the old lady seems to disappear, but then I see her again. 'Mrs Craven, you forgot your sticks.'

She hurries towards the front door and fumbles with the lock. 'Remember, dear, never believe malicious gossip...think for yourself and you'll bloom into a young woman with inner beauty.' She turns and smiles before saying, 'It's what's on the inside that matters. Good luck in your biology test.'

As soon as Mrs Craven pulls the door open, a flash of white light blinds me. I splutter as my breath is snatched from my body, causing me to drop the walking sticks. Then, my body is overwhelmed by a strong pulling sensation, as if I'm being forced out of one realm into another. My mouth opens to scream, but I make no sound. Overcome with dizziness, I close my eyelids. *Stay awake...please stay...*Moments later, my fading world turns black...

'Stacey...Stacey, get up.'

Someone tugs my arm. My whole body feels laden with lead. My heart is pounding as I look up at Cameron who's trying to pull me off the damp ground.

'There's no point sitting there in the rain,' says Cameron, 'Craven slammed the door in our faces, she isn't going to open it again.'

'Good,' interjects Tom. 'I never wanted to go in the creepy old woman's house anyway.'

I feel a surge of anger...*creepy old woman!* 'Don't you dare call Mrs Craven creepy!' I shove Cameron away and stand up. 'She's a wonderful, intelligent–'

Cameron's eyebrows shoot up. 'You were the one calling her names this morning–'

Tom interrupts, 'Ugly old Craven slams the door in our faces, me and Cameron run and fall down two great big, waterlogged holes in her garden, and when we finally clamber out' – he points to his muddy clothes to emphasise his point – 'we find *you* passed out on her doorstep. And now you think that she's...*wonderful?*'

I stare at them. 'But Mrs Craven did let me inside...she showed me all her beautiful flowers...'

Cameron picks my coat up from the path and passes it to me. 'I think you've hit your head, Stacy.' Drizzle dances around his concerned face.

I shake my head. 'I don't understand...I've been talking to Mrs Craven for ages...she taught me all about photosynthesis and pollination and...' I slip my arms into my damp coat and pull it back on. 'That's why I wasn't wearing my coat...I took it off in the old lady's house, but she passed it back to me before...' I turn and knock on Mrs Craven's front door. 'Mrs Craven! *Please*, open the door! It's Stacey Smyth!' I knock harder.

Cameron grabs my arm. 'Forget it, Stacey...she isn't going to let us in.'

I turn on hearing the gate thump at the end of the old lady's path. 'Stacey!'

'Oh, yeah,' says Cameron, 'I forgot to mention, we phoned your mum.'

Mum staggers down the slippery path. 'Why didn't you come straight home from school? You shouldn't have gone to Mrs Craven's house first!'

I sigh. 'I didn't think coming here earlier would make much difference. One minute you can't wait to get me here, the next you're trying to stop...' My voice trails off as soon as I realise Mum has tears in her eyes. 'What's the matter?'

Mum sniffs. 'It's Mrs Craven...she passed away this morning.'

I shake my head. I look at Cameron and Tom. 'No, Mum, she's alive...I spoke to her only a few minutes ago...' I gulp. 'She showed me all her beautiful flowers.'

Mum grabs my hand and says, 'Stacey, Mrs Craven never let anyone near her flowers, and she's been too ill to tend them herself for months...'

Cameron interjects, 'But Tom and me saw her, too...I think...Didn't we, Tom?'

Wide-eyed, Tom nods and shrugs his shoulders at the same time. 'Well, we saw the door open and assumed it was the old woman.'

Mum fumbles in her pocket and pulls out some keys. 'Mrs Craven was a lovely lady – misunderstood by so many people.'

Still dazed, I ask, 'Why do you have her keys?'

'I've been checking on her for a while now,' answered Mum. 'No one else would help her...all the neighbours are silly enough to believe all the horrible rumours. Some were stupid enough to believe that one look from Mrs Craven would turn you to *stone*!'

I cringe, knowing I believed the rumours, too.

Mum continued, 'Mrs Craven should've done more to stop the rumours from spreading.' She opened the old lady's door. 'As time passed, the tales grew more and more ridiculous.'

Cameron and I look at Tom who lowers his head to stare at the path. I wonder if he fears his rumours spreading out of control, too?

I walk in after Mum. It's the same dingy, sparsely furnished room. *I can't be imagining it...I've been here before...I have met Mrs Craven!* Then I notice her walking sticks on the floor...I turn to look at Cameron, Tom and my mother all staring back at me. 'This is where I dropped the old lady's walking sticks.' I charge through the room past Mrs Craven's pot table and open the door to the next room to show them her beautiful plants. Instead of the intoxicating scent of flowers, I'm overcome by the pungent smell of mould emanating from the dark, chilly room. I turn on the light. 'I don't understand...' I head towards the smaller room where Mrs Craven showed me her cuttings. I stare in bewilderment... at an army of brown, lifeless cuttings whose crispy leaves now litter the dry soil. A lump rises in my throat. *What happened to the beautiful flowers?* 'I – I would've watered them for her, if I'd known...she loved her flowers...'

Mum hugs me. 'It's not your fault, Stacey. She always refused any offer of help with her flowers.'

Over Mum's shoulder I notice a single green cutting planted in a separate pot. I gently move away from her and reach out. *It's the cutting Mrs Craven planted with me...I'm sure it is!*

Mum smiles. 'Mrs Craven would be more than happy for you to take the pot. She always wished she'd had a child of her own to pass her knowledge of plants on to before she died.'

I clutch the pot to my chest. *Whether I've imagined meeting Mrs Craven or not, I'm going to make sure this plant doesn't die like all her others.* My eyes glaze over.

Mum links her arm with mine. 'Let's go home.'

The next day, Tom volunteered to join Mr Drayton's lunchtime detention. He also fixed the rumours about his mother's sickness. And at the end of the week, Cameron, Tom and I all passed our biology retakes...and I ended up with the highest marks in the class! Mum was ecstatic!

I have to accept that nobody will ever believe I saw Mrs Craven that day. Whether my encounter with her was real or not, my outlook on life has changed forever.

As the cutting grew, I transferred it into a larger pot. It seemed quite happy growing on our kitchen windowsill...Mum was convinced it was because she talked to it...*she's so weird, but that's why I love her.*

A few months after Mrs Craven died, in early spring, a bud appeared on the plant. Mum and I waited patiently for the flower to open. Then, on the morning of my final biology exam, Mum woke me early...

'Stacey! It's opened!'

I dart down the stairs and into the kitchen.

'Stacey, look, it's a beautiful pink rose. It smells' – Mum inhales a deep breath – 'gorgeous.' She lifts the plant pot and waves the scent under my nose.

It's exactly the same as the rose Mrs Craven showed me. 'I know this flower's name...she called it...Rosa!'

Mum smiles. 'That's sweet, dear, naming the flower after Mrs Craven...I had no idea you knew her first name was Rosa?'

My eyes widen as a ghostly whisper leaves my lips, 'I – I didn't...'

A CURIOUS FIRST DAY

S C Dann

'How do you know I'm mad?' said Alice.

'You must be,' said the cat, 'or you wouldn't have come here.'

— Lewis Carroll

A CURIOUS FIRST DAY

My pace slows as I watch the other kids pouring through the school gates. My palms are sweaty and my heart is pounding. Every single one of them has probably grown up in the same neighbourhood. They almost certainly all started the school at the same time.

This is my first day.

Feeling sick and dizzy, I turn to look at Mum still waiting in the car. Her features are clouded by my watery vision. I bet she wishes I'd be more like my younger sister who skipped happily through the school gate a few moments ago. Alice makes friends easily. She'll talk to anyone – even her pet rabbit! I'm sure she thinks the rabbit's talking back to her sometimes!

If I had her confidence, I might be able to see this change in our lives as a wonderful adventure – instead, I feel as if I'm boarding a ship that's almost certainly going to sink.

Mum gestures at me to move forward...I hadn't realised I'd stopped. I place one tentative foot in front of the other, taking deep breaths, which does little to calm my nerves or the frenzied butterflies trapped inside me. *Why did we have to move? I liked my last school. These kids look so...different.* My thoughts are interrupted when I reach the gates and a group of boys about my age stop chatting and turn to stare at me. *Shall I ignore them? They're probably thinking I'm a short, stuck-up boy who thinks he's too good for this school...well, that's NOT what I'm thinking!* One of the boys with cropped hair curls his lips into a strange grin. *Is he smiling or sneering at me?* I exhale. *My friends at my last school were right – this place is a nightmare! Well, if any of these fools think they're going to scare me...* Head down, I hurry past them through the gate. *I hate it here already!*

I follow the mob through some double doors to face rows of scratched and dented lockers. Trying to ignore the deafening clatter of metal locker doors and chatter, I delve into my trouser pocket and pull out my key to check its number. My parents had already visited the school – *without me* – to see if it was 'suitable' and had made sure I was given a locker key in advance.

I take a deep breath and stand still, observing the mayhem. I see no sign of my sister. Some of the children are forcing their bags into their tiny lockers while others are laughing, chatting and messing about with their friends. A cluster of boys falls to the floor play fighting after one of their rucksacks is tossed into the air. It hits a girl's back. Interrupted mid-yawn, she turns and squeals at them, lobbing the rucksack straight back at the tangled mass of scruffy uniformed bodies, rolling over the dusty floor.

A tall girl with blonde ponytails knocks into me as she rushes past, looking at her watch. 'I'm late!' she mutters. Without apologising, she scurries off and disappears into the throng.

So, this is the 'best' school in the area for kids who are interested in drama? THIS is the school Mum has spent the last week trying to convince me will be better than my last school! My face contorts. She's been going on and on about the school's upcoming production, telling me about the two performances that the children here are deciding between. I rub my clammy palms down the sides of my trousers. *Choices...decisions...I wish I could've decided which school I'd go to instead of some stupid play! As if I'll have any influence over which play they'll choose anyway!*

I push my fingers through the knots in my curly hair, straighten my posture and wait for someone sensible to come to my aid, to lead me away from this chaotic scene. My parents told me I'd be met by a chaperone who was supposed to ease me into life at Blunderbrooks High School... *Well, I can't see anyone waiting to –*

'Hi,' says someone with a deep voice. 'I'm Tobias.'

I whip round and strain my neck to look up at a spotty, tall, chubby boy who gives me a weird smirk. *Oh no! It's the grinning boy at the gate! He's* – I gulp – *huge...*

'Are you' – he racks his *tiny* brain for my name – 'Batter, Ratter, Hatter...Gatter?' He pulls the bottom of his 'white' shirt over his round belly and tucks it into the front of his mud-stained trousers. 'Gatter...that's right.' He scratches his temple.

I nod. *It's Thomas Gatter, actually* – but I stare at him without uttering a word. *He looks and acts like a stupid troll!*

'Your locker number's forty-two, ain't it?'

'Yes.' *He can't even talk properly!*

The boy looks at me with a vacant expression.

I suppress a sigh. 'Yes...it's forty-two,' I repeat a little louder. My voice cracks. *Can he hear me above all this noise?*

The boy trudges towards the heaving mob, which engulfs the bottom half of his body. *Did I offend him?* I bite my bottom lip. *I answered his question...*His fat head and broad shoulders bob around as he jostles for space among the bustling bodies. *The teachers at my last school wouldn't have put up with disorder like this! I'm not going to survive a single day here!*

I take a deep breath and raise my chin. *I'm a decent, well-educated boy...I refuse to be intimidated by a bunch of –*

'Hey! Gatter!'

Troll Boy is gesturing at me to join him. He cups his hands round his mouth and bellows, 'Locker forty-two is 'ere!'

Head held high, I walk towards him, zigzagging through the party of mad animals.

Hands shaking, I reach up on tiptoes and force my key into locker forty-two. *Very funny...give the new short kid the top locker!*

The door swings open and a cascade of empty drinks cans comes crashing down on top of me! Disorientated by the wave of clattering cans, I wince as a sharp pain shoots across the top of my forehead. I wobble. Flashes of white light zip before my unfocused eyes. Searing pains spread through my head like wildfire. I reach out to steady myself. But my body feels too heavy for my weakening skeleton. The intense brightness turns into an array of twinkling stars, growing dimmer as they fade into the looming darkness. I hear my own distressed calls echoing through my brain. *Will no one help me?* Lost and alone, I sink deeper and deeper into the black abyss of silence...

'Help him...!' I hear a girl shout.

My eyes ping open.

'All right!' says a boy. 'I must've forgotten to empty...I didn't mean...bit of fun.'

I shake my head, hearing only parts of their muffled speech because the noise of the cans is still rattling in my ears. Then, someone grasps my arms and pulls me to my feet. My eyes widen as soon as I realise it's Troll Boy. I twist myself free and stumble through the clattering cans. I grab a swinging locker door to steady myself. The metal digs into my palm as I gaze at the crowd that has gathered around me.

Within seconds, I'm engulfed by thunderous laughter. Adrenaline races through my body. I can feel my cheeks burning. I tremble with anger, wishing for another rush of cans to fall and cover my entire body to hide my humiliation.

'Sorry, mate, but you've got to admit that that was funny!' Troll Boy wheezes with laughter.

I glare at him, wishing I were a beam of sunlight that could turn his *stupid* troll body into stone. He stumbles backwards, falling over his huge feet as he points at me laughing with tears in his eyes.

I hate him! Kicking the cans out of my way, I reach up, throw my bag into my locker and yank the key, which is still attached by the key chain to my trousers, from the lock. I blink rapidly. My blurred vision gives me the strange illusion that my key is more than three times the size it was before. I shove it in my pocket. Maybe it's because I feel ten times smaller than I did this morning.

The laughter continues as I kick the clattering cans out of my way and stagger off to find the school office. *There must be someone other than Troll Boy who can show me around the school.*

Each step forward aggravates my throbbing head. I feel around my scalp and discover the pain is coming from a tender, raised bump. I flatten my hair down to cover it. A wave of nausea causes me to stagger sideways and fall against a door, which swings open. I stumble inside the room, which is lined with mirrors, and stare at my reflection through misty eyes.

I know I'm crying, but I can't help it. If I could shed enough tears, I'd cry a sea of them to swallow me up and wash me away. My thoughts seem so vivid, I'm sure I can feel freezing water swirling around my feet...my legs...my waist...my chest...My breathing quickens as the water begins to bubble and foam around my neck, lapping against my cheeks. The water covers my mouth, reducing my screams to a gush of bubbles – precious air...

Then, someone grabs my arm and shouts, 'Turn the tap off!'

I'm shoved out of the way and the tap is turned off. Water is gushing over the sink on to the tiled floor. I step back and take in my surroundings...*I must be in the boys' toilets.* I stagger backwards. *I don't remember –*

'What are you doing in the girls' bogs?'

I look up at Troll Boy. 'I don't know...' I rub my fingers over the bump on my head.

He leans forward and examines the side of my head. 'I'm sorry about the cans in your locker, mate.'

I stare back at him, clenching my teeth...*I don't care about the cans...Do you honestly think I can't handle a few empty cans dropping on my head!* I bite my lip, controlling the urge to communicate my true feelings.

Without warning he grabs my arm and pulls me towards the door. 'Let's get out of here before anyone sees us.' My feet are sliding through the water like a novice ice skater. The door swings open before we reach it and slams against the wall.

My heart sinks.

Two girls step back in bewilderment.

The shorter one with the mousy-brown hair and beady eyes blurts, 'Have you lost your way, *new boy?*' Her nose scrunches up and twitches like a mouse before she breaks into a wide-mouthed yawn. 'You should tell someone about that knock to his head, Tobias.' Her eyes point to me.

The taller one with long blonde hair tied in two bunches adds, 'He's been swaying all over the place like a drunk since those cans fell on him!'

No I'm not, I think. I start scanning my surroundings...*everything around me is in perfect focus.* My cloudy eyes widen as the tiles near my feet start to bob up and down on the flooded floor. I blink rapidly.

The girl continues, 'Look!' – she points, stamping her foot on the floating tiles – 'he's flooded the toilet floor! He's delirious, I tell you.' She hurries past me, her ponytails bouncing like floppy rabbit ears, and brushes past Troll Boy. 'You're going to be in *so* much trouble when the teachers find out what you've done to him, Tobias.' She hops around the water to turn off the tap.

I – I thought Troll Boy already turned the tap off? Or was that another sink? I wince as a pain shoots through the bump on my head, sending a curvy line of stars floating across my vision. *I'm confused...*

Tobias interjects, 'It was only supposed to be a bit of fun...to help ease him into life here.'

Floppy Hair adds, 'If the new boy carries on like this, everyone will think he's *mad!'* She looks at her watch and mutters, 'Look, we're already late! And this mess is going to make us even later for our first lesson!'

'You'd better keep a close eye on him,' insists Mousy Hair. 'He doesn't even know the difference between the girls' and boys' toilets!' Her sleepy rodent eyes look me up and down. 'You'll have to own up to your stupid prank eventually, Tobias, look at him!'

Troll Boy interjects, 'Stop worrying, he'll be fine. We just need to find a way to put his weird behaviour to good use...I'll work it out...eventually.' He chuckles and jabs me on my upper arm. 'I think I'm going to like you, my new mad mate!'

My shoulder thuds against the tiled wall, breaking my fall. *Great! That's all I need...I have no desire to be in the constant company of an overweight dummy who –*

'Come on...*Triton*,' calls Troll Boy, 'We need to get you to your first lesson...geography with Mrs Royal...you'll *love* her! She teaches drama too. I hear it's your favourite subject, so you need to try your best to impress her if you want a part in the production.' He looks at the flooded floor and giggles. 'You can take a swim later! Bye, girls! Come on, Triton!' he calls, slipping out of the toilets.

'Great!' exclaims Floppy. 'We'll clean up the mess then shall we?'

Yawning, Mousy grabs a wad of paper towels from the dispenser.

Triton? One little incident with water and he's calling me a mythological creature of the sea...a merman! I stumble past Mousy who is spreading paper towels over the flooded floor, and follow Troll Boy into the deserted corridor. *Some merman...I can't even swim!*

Panting, I try to keep up with Troll Boy thundering ahead. I can hear his laughter increasing in volume, echoing back as if I've already been lured into his hollow troll cave.

Seconds later, the floor rises in front of me. *What's happening?* My heartbeat quickens. I slow my pace. I turn, my eyes shifting from left to right – *the walls...they're closing in on me, too!* I spin round to find Troll Boy. But I can't see him...

Arms outstretched, I stagger from one side of the narrowing corridor to the other, inhaling sharp, panicked breaths. *Is the space around me getting smaller or am I getting bigger?* My eyes spin in their sockets. *Where is he?* My thudding head is making me feel increasingly giddy and confused. I turn again...but I still can't see him anywhere. The walls are moving closer and closer!

'Troll Boy!' I holler.

I gasp as my breath is snatched from my body. I'm lifted off the ground, feet swinging like a man hanging from a noose. My shirt collar is tightening around my neck.

'What did ya call me?' bellows Troll Boy.

He's going to kill me! His bloodshot eyes are in line with mine, merging together in my watery vision like the single eye of a giant Cyclops. *Who looks like a mythological creature now?* 'Put – me – down!'

'Okay...okay, calm down.' He places me back down on the floor and says, 'Troll Boy...I like it...it makes me sound...tough.' A gormless smile spreads across his face. 'A nickname like that could help me stand out when Mrs Royal picks the leading roles in the play.'

Feeling dizzy and disorientated, I slump down. Troll Boy's massive shadow swallows my body as he stands over me, framed by the glare of sunlight from the window behind him, which, unfortunately, fails to turn him into a stone troll. I squint up at his features, faded by the bright light, while he continues to waffle on about the parts in the two productions he'd like to play. I hear almost nothing he says.

I begin to feel giddy again, even though the walls and the floor are no longer closing in. *Why do I keep imagining these strange things? I must be ill.* My mouth begins to water. *Oh no! I think I'm going to spew!* Troll Boy is too wrapped up in his own conversation to notice me. I swallow, taking quick, shallow breaths. *Please...don't vomit!* My diaphragm begins to rock back and forth. I feel as if I'm going to faint. Sweat begins to ooze from every pore. I shut my eyes...*I wish I was back home.* My mind is whirling like a ship being sucked into a gigantic whirlpool, as if the mythological monster Charybdis is pulling me closer to its swirling vortex of doom. I shudder as burning acid spills into my mouth. I see Troll Boy rushing towards me. My heavy eyelids flutter. Then, my world is blotted by the rapid spread of inky darkness...

I'm woken with a start. My chest thumps against the desk in front of me, making my chair wobble. My eyes dart back and forth – I'm in a classroom? *How did I get here?* I check the floor. *Did I throw up?* Thankfully, I can't see any vomit.

'Gatter!' shouts a high-pitched voice.

I sit up, blinking rapidly. I'm alerted to two short, podgy women with wild, curly, ginger hair standing at the front of the classroom, pointing their fingers at me. The two hazy women, each wearing a bright red dress, begin to merge, forming one clearer figure who is now stomping towards me.

My heart flutters with dread. *Oh No! What have I done now?* Her fists are clenched beside her body, and her puffed-up face looks like a shiny, red balloon about to burst. I shuffle in my chair as she halts in front of me. Her scarf falls from her neck and floats down on to my desk, spreading its white rose print like a newly bloomed border.

Mrs Royal snatches the scarf and waves it at me. 'I told you' – spit and blasts of hot air are spurting from her mouth – 'to stand at the back of the classroom with *your hands on your head!'* After expelling so much angry air, her face sags and shrivels like a deflated balloon. She wraps her scarf round her neck – the white roses on it clashing with her red puffy face like two contrasting flowerbeds – and stomps back to the front of the class.

I scan the room. Every child is sniggering at me, including Troll Boy who is sitting at his desk in the farthest corner of the room. He puts his thumb up to me, but I ignore him and look away. I want to ask this angry teacher: *What have I done?* However, it's quite clear that I'd be wasting my time with this irrational woman, so I stand up and start moving to the back of the classroom. I stumble past Floppy Hair, chewing her gum.

'Rebecca!' shouts the teacher.

Floppy's eyes flick away from me. She jolts upright in her chair and stops chewing. 'Yes, Mrs Royal?'

The teacher hisses, 'Spit that disgusting thing in the bin and stand at the back of the classroom with your *hands on your head!* You've already been given detention today for being late for class...you'll end up in detention tomorrow lunchtime, too, if you're not careful!'

I spot Mousy Hair as I make my way to the back of the classroom. She finishes yawning and smiles at me. *Why are they trying to be so friendly, they don't even know me?* Confused, I look away and focus on the back wall ahead, which is covered in posters of different continents. *I'm clearly in the geography room, but...how did I get here? Who brought me here?* I rub my head...*I can't remember...*

Floppy shoves her desk forward and trudges the long way round the classroom towards the bin. As she passes me, she reaches into her mouth, pinches the gum she's holding between her rabbit-like teeth and pulls. It stretches from her pouting lips like a serpent's tongue.

If anyone ever needs to cast a mythological creature with a tongue like a snake in a play, she'll be perfect! Any other notable talents...none!

I reach the back of the classroom and place my hands on my head, facing a map of The Americas – a land for dreamers. I wish I could jump into it and disappear...but I'm stuck in this nightmare of a school!

After about five minutes, my arms feel as heavy as lead. My shoulder muscles are taut and aching as if I've been weightlifting all morning. *How am I going to keep my hands on my head for the entire lesson?*

I glance sideways. Floppy is standing at the back of the classroom a few paces away from me now. She's looking from her watch to the map of Asia, sighing with impatience.

Seconds later, we both jolt upright when Mrs Royal shouts at another girl called Mia, ordering her to stand at the back of the class for talking. The teacher's piercing voice triggers another stabbing pain in my head.

I hear some dainty footsteps, and then Mousy appears beside me. She yawns, drops her forehead against the map of Africa and her eyes snap shut. Her breathing instantly becomes slower and deeper. *Has she gone to sleep?*

'Tobias!' Mrs Royal roars.

Mousy's droopy eyes ping open for a few seconds before closing again.

The teacher continues to shout, 'Take that ridiculous grin off your face and stand at the back of the classroom with your *hands on your head!*'

I can hear Troll Boy chuckling as he trudges across the classroom to stand in front of Australia, beside Floppy. I glance over and he nods at me, smiling. *Stop smiling at me!* I frown back...*I'm sure he was sitting in the opposite corner of the room...why did he come from that direction?*

My aching arms finally lose their fight with gravity and drop to my sides as Mrs Royal screams out another name.

Mousy's eyes stay closed this time.

'Toby Dunn! Stand at the back of the class with your *hands on your head!'*

I clench my teeth and give my arms a quick shake while the teacher orders the boy to join our motley crew, forcing us all to face the dangers of the world's oceans together, whether we want to or not. My eyes roam across the maps. *We'll have enough sailors to travel to all the continents of the world by the time this teacher's finished recruiting!*

As soon as the blood has pumped into my arms again, I roll my shoulders forward and put my hands back on my head. Standing in one place for so long is making me feel really light-headed.

Tobias is smiling broadly as he turns to greet the newest recruit, Toby, with a high five. *He's so dumb! We're being punished and he's acting as if we're all standing here because we've been picked for the leading roles in a play!* My eyes widen as I look up at the new boy in our line-up. Mouth open, I stare at him squeezing his fat body next to me in front of the map of Europe. My hands drop to my sides and my head flicks sideways to look back at Tobias, and then again at Toby...*I'm seeing double!* I squeeze my eyes shut and inhale a deep breath. When my eyes ping open, I look left, then right again. *No! No! There can't be two of them! Tobias the first Troll Boy and Toby the next...What's happening?*

My head whips one way, then the other, which sends my dizziness into overdrive. *I'm sure there's only one of them...they'll converge to form one troll boy any minute now...like the two images of Mrs Royal. I'm seeing double because I'm feeling giddy from standing here for too long...that's all...*

The first Troll Boy leans sideways and whispers to me, 'This is Toby Dunn, my twin brother.' He points at his mirror image.

The next Troll Boy whispers, 'This is Tobias Dunn, my twin brother. He also points at his mirror image.

There really are two of them! My – head – hurts!

'Gaaaaatter!'

Mrs Royal shouts out my name. As her voice reverberates through my ears, it transforms into a tune that sounds more like the enchanting voice of a Siren rising from the depths of the sea to lure a ship and its crew towards the rocky coastline and certain death. Pressing my palms over my ears, I shake my woozy head and stagger backwards. *Why is the room rocking like the deck of a ship?* I swallow. *What's happening?*

Wrapped in a darkening cloud, I stumble backwards as a gust of salty air whistles round my body, ruffling my trousers, shirt and blazer. I try to regain focus, but the classroom's a blur. The rocking motion increases. I stagger over the tilting floor, lose my balance and smack into a wooden pole. I stumble back and look up at a huge mast adorned with canvases, flapping wildly in the turbulent wind. *Am I on a...ship?* I turn and duck, but I'm too late – water cascades over me, knocking me on to the slippery wooden planks, which are awash with ice-cold frothy water. *I AM on the deck of a ship!* Shivering violently, I pull myself to my knees and sweep my saturated hair from my eyes, which are already stinging from the salty water. *I have to get up...I must steer the ship away from the rocks!*

I scramble across the slippery wooden planks, flinching every time the freezing water lashes at the deck and my trembling body. *I must reach the helm...I need to take control of the ship's wheel!*

The vessel begins to dip and spin. Teeth chattering, I look up at the creaking mast and the sails thrashing in the turbulent air above me. Then, the ship changes direction. The jolt sends me stumbling into the wooden mast. Doubled over, I push away and stagger backwards, hugging my ribs. I squeeze my eyes shut and wince as the pain spreads through them like a raging fire.

Moments later, the ship jolts, twists and rears like an enraged bull. The vibrations ricochet through my body. I stumble across the deck like a puppet with severed strings. My screams tear at my dry throat, but my desperate cries are drowned-out by the sounds of creaking wood, whistling wind and the gushing and hissing of the merciless seawater, attacking me from all sides.

The ship jolts again, harder this time, smashing into something with immense force. I fall face down on the wooden planks. Spluttering and groaning, I tuck myself into a ball. As the ship begins to list, I slide across the bumpy deck and hit into the curved sidewall. I shudder, listening to the cracking and splintering of wood. My heart is thudding. *We must've hit the rocks!*

Within seconds, I hear the roar of rushing water. *'Nooooo!'* Each panicked breath stabs at my lungs like a knife as I watch a torrent of seawater gushing through an enormous jagged hole in the side of the ship. *'Please, help me! I can't swim!'* My eyes snap shut. I inhale deep, panicked breaths.

'Off to the head!'

I stop shaking and freeze, holding my breath...I can still hear Mrs Royal's voice ringing in my ears. I open my misty eyes and scan my surroundings.

'Ouch!' I flinch, releasing a sudden rush of air from my lungs. The skin on my upper arms pinches as I'm pulled to my feet. *'Quickly'* – I stop speaking and pant like an overheated dog – 'we need to get *off* the ship and on to the lifeboats...before we all *drown*! *Please, before it's too late! I can't swim!'* I exclaim. As I rise, I can see the hazy outline of Mrs Royal pointing at the door. *Why is SHE on the ship?*

'Off to the head!' she repeats.

I glance left, then right. The two Troll Boys, one on each arm, are staring at me in bewilderment as they lift me off the floor.

'What ship?' whispers one Troll Boy. He looks at his brother. '*What* is the new boy talking about? He's *mad...*he thinks he's on a ship.'

The other one whispers back, '*A ship?* So, that's what all the thrashing around was about. He's completely *mad*. As mad as a hatter.'

The first boy nods and agrees, 'As mad as a hatter.'

They begin to shuffle me forward. My feet are dangling between both boys as they drag me along, stepping over some of the unoccupied tables and chairs, which appear to have been knocked over by someone. *Tables? Chairs? Why are they on the ship?*

I try to wriggle free from my captors, but they tighten their hold on my arms. Disorientated and woozy from the pain in my head, I blink rapidly, looking from one boy to the next. *I knew it! They're not trolls...they're both one-eyed, giant Cyclops!* 'Help me!' Spit bubbles inside my mouth as I continue to struggle. I look over my shoulder as they drag me towards the door. 'Let – go – of – me!'

I can see a row of children standing at the back of the room and few still sitting at their desks. They're all staring back at me in confusion – some of them are sniggering, too. '*Please*, save me!' I shout.

I'm hustled through the door. Saliva escapes my gaping mouth and dribbles down my chin. I groan in frustration – I'm unable to wipe it away because my arms are being held down.

One of the Troll Boys says, 'How are we supposed to calm him down?'

The other one adds, 'How should I know? Let's just get him away from Mrs Royal.'

My throat tightens as my gurgling groans turn into quivering sobs. I look up at my captors...both of them appear to have two eyes again! I let out an involuntary whine. *I need to STOP IMAGINING THINGS...I'm not being dragged away by a pair of giant Cyclops! I'm not even on a ship! I'm still in this...HORRIBLE SCHOOL being manhandled by two stupid fat boys! I want to go home!*

My eyelids flutter as I struggle to cope with the continuous thudding pain in my head. I inhale deeply, listening to the boys' voices echoing in my brain like trapped memories...

'We can't take him there now,' says Troll Boy One.

'Why not?' asks Troll Boy Two. 'The water might bring him back to his senses...you know...calm him down. It might help soothe the bump on his head, too. Unless you've any better ideas?'

'But we're supposed to take him to the headmaster. And what happens if we throw him in and he *can't* swim?'

'Everyone can swim...can't they?

'I suppose we'll find out.'

'If not, we can teach him...together!'

'Yes, let's teach him together!'

Each rasping breath dries my already parched throat. *Where – are – they – taking me? I don't want them to help me, or teach me anything!*

I must be getting heavier. My shoes are dragging over the floor surfaces...smooth...squeaky...sticky...I want to pull myself free, but my muscles are weak and unresponsive. The floor surfaces change from hard, to scratchy, to bumpy...

My mind is wandering through an endless maze of unconnected thoughts. *One minute I'm convinced that I'm on a sailing ship and in the presence of mythological creatures. Then, it's as if I've fallen into a huge hole and I'm trapped in a dream with nothing but a bunch of mad individuals for companionship! Have I lost all sense of reality? Or am I dreaming...trapped in my subconscious?*

The Troll Boys' voices become more distant, echoing through my muffled ears in deep incoherent rumbles. I feel a sudden change in temperature and humidity, which zaps what little energy I have left. I give up trying to break free and wilt like a dehydrated plant as they let go of me and place me on a cold, hard floor.

I choose to ignore the sound of lapping water and the ripples of glistening light, flickering across the wall in front of me. I won't be fooled again – I know it's only the subconscious parts of my mind playing tricks on me.

Moments later, I'm lifted off the floor by my limbs. My body rocks in mid-air, swinging back and forth over an imaginary blue hue, sparkling like thousands of diamonds below me.

Up...down...up...down...up...

'Are you sure we're doing the right thing?' I hear one of the Troll Boys ask.

The other replies, 'A bit of water won't hurt him.'

I'm mesmerised by the undulating rivulets, reflecting over the ceiling as I continue to swing higher and higher...

Up...down...up...down...up...

'Ahhhhh!' My body is released! I'm flying through the air!

I feel free and weightless as I float like a butterfly released from its chrysalis. Then, I feel the sudden pull of gravity. *'Heeeeelp!'* I begin to drop like a strange talking caterpillar who realises he hasn't metamorphosed yet.

SPLASH!

I gasp as I hit the cool water. *Oh no! The water...it's real!* The crushing pressure surrounding my sinking body suppresses my attempts to scream. *Help! I can't swim!* My limbs move frantically, creating a whirl of bubbles. Cheeks bulging, I stop the remaining air in my lungs from escaping by sealing my lips tightly together as I spin like a disorientated fish with damaged fins. My lungs are expanding...*I've only a few seconds before...*My eyes dart from left to right, following the rising bubbles in the water like two fish in a panicked shoal. *Where's the surface?* Then, my balloon lungs burst, releasing a blinding mass of bubbles. My nose and mouth begin to fill with water. My thrashing limbs become heavy and slow. Eyelids half closed, I stare out at the shimmering flashes of light, listening to the muffled voices above me, calling my name. Then, a blanket of darkening shadows shrouds my glistening world as I sink to the depths of my subconscious...

My cheeks are stinging...I can hear voices echoing all around me...A rush of choking water rises up my throat, spilling into my mouth. I jolt forward, spluttering. Water spurts from my mouth in intermittent bursts. I gasp for air, but my lungs feel like sodden sandbags in the wake of a flood.

My body begins to relax as I inhale injections of air. I open my misty eyes and look up at the worried faces staring down at me. My tender chest feels as if I've been trapped underground for hours. But, my mind feels much clearer now, as if I've finally managed to sail the treacherous journey back from a world of mad dreams to the realms of reality.

I lift my head as a door slams. A draught snakes over me, making me shudder. I turn on to my side. *Why are my clothes sticking to my body?* I look down at my uniform, and then scan my surroundings. *I'm fully clothed and soaking wet, and I'm lying at the edge of a...swimming pool?*

I can hear hurried footsteps approaching behind me.

'Don't worry, it's all under control, Miss, he's method acting,' Tobias blurts, as the footsteps get closer. He grabs a handful of his shirt and wrings out the water, which drips on to the tiled floor.

It's Mrs Royal. She steps in front of me with her hands on her hips, glaring at Tobias.

Toby interjects, 'You know, Miss, he's one of those actors who like to stay in character' – he pauses to make eye contact with his brother – 'even when they're not *actually* acting.' He looks as drenched as his brother, standing with his legs apart and his arms slightly raised at his sides.

Mrs Royal switches her glare to Toby.

Both of them must've jumped into the pool, too. Did they jump in to save me?

Tobias adds, 'Can't you see, Mrs Royal, he's desperate for a part in one of the plays. He thinks he's Sinbad. All that strange behaviour in your geography class was all part of his plan – he wanted to impress you with his method acting.'

The boys lean forward, each grabbing one of my arms, and pull me into a sitting position. *What are they talking about? I wasn't method acting...*I go to speak, but Toby crouches in front of me, blocking the teacher's view, and gently places his clammy hand over my mouth. My eyes widen as he smiles at me, pressing the forefinger of his other hand against his lips, telling me to hush. He whispers into my ear, 'Just play along, mate...if we stick together we might all end up with a part in the school play.'

What are they up to? How are these idiots going to help me get a role –?'

'To start with, we thought' – Tobias encourages Mrs Royal to turn and face the pool, so that he can lightly kick Toby's hand away from my mouth – 'he'd make a great Sinbad in your preferred choice for this year's production...So he jumped in the pool as part of a test...to show us that he can swim like any good sailor should.'

Toby stands up, rubbing his arm and nods in agreement. 'But, clearly, he can't swim because we had to jump in and pull him out. So, it's quite obvious he'd make a *terrible* sailor. But we think Gatter's proved that he's crazy enough to play the Mad Hatter in *Alice's Adventures in Wonderland* – the second choice for the production this year. What do you think, Mrs Royal? He did jump into a swimming pool, knowing that he couldn't swim because he wanted a part so desperately.' He chuckles. 'He'd be Gatter the Hatter.'

My eyes flick from Toby and Tobias to Mrs Royal. *They're bonkers if they think she'll believe any of that nonsense...* The teacher stares past everyone in deep thought. *Is she actually stupid enough to believe them?* I feel a surge of hope as she continues to ponder. *She's actually considering it? If they manage to pull this off, I – I'll be the luckiest kid ever! I'd do anything to play that role...Please, please say yes...*

Mrs Royal frowns. 'So all that crazy I'm-on-a-sinking-ship behaviour in my geography class, including the knocking over of tables and chairs, was the new boy attempting to impress me with his acting skills?' She taps a finger on her chin and mumbles, 'He was method acting...It's a bit extreme...But...'

It's working...she's falling for it...

Then, Floppy Hair appears. She looks down at me sitting on the floor. 'What difference would it make if he can swim or not – we wouldn't be performing the play anywhere near any water!' she exclaims.

Oh no! Shut her up...she's going to ruin everything!

She continues, 'And he's *not* method acting – he's behaving like this because he got hit on the head by a full can of–'

So, one of the cans in my locker was full of drink when it fell on me... that's why I have a bump on my head, and why I've been feeling and acting so weird.

'Ouch!' Floppy stops talking, grits her teeth and lifts one leg. 'Toby!' she curses. 'Why did you tread on my...' She remains on one leg, rubbing the top of her foot.

I hear Toby whisper to her, 'Start hopping.' He grabs her hand and gently encourages her to move up and down. 'Look, Mrs Royal, Rebecca would make a brilliant White Rabbit or March Hare – she hops just like one.'

My mind flashes back to her stretched chewing gum tongue in the geography lesson, and I wonder whether she'd make a better mythological snake-like creature from Sinbad – a Naga – than a cute fluffy rabbit.

Floppy stops hopping and looks straight at Mrs Royal. She winks at Toby and smiles, suddenly aware of the boys' game plan, 'I would' – she starts bouncing up and down on two feet, ponytails bobbing like floppy ears – 'I'd make a brilliant White Rabbit or March Hare!' She bounces towards Mousy and grabs her arm to pull her closer. 'Mrs Royal, if I'm in the play, can Mia be in the play, too? I promise – I'll make sure we're never late for rehearsals.' Breathless, she stops bouncing.

Mousy turns round, yawning. 'But what part would I play?' She rubs her sleepy eyes, swaying as if she might fall on me. 'I'm not sure I really like acting that much.'

They're suggesting acting parts for everyone! I stare at them in disbelief. *I can't believe it! If their plan works, I could land my dream role as the Mad Hatter! And all my weird behaviour, which would've made me look a complete freak on my first day, would be excused because of my love of acting.* My thoughts feel clearer than they've felt all day...*Throwing me into a cold swimming pool must've been exactly what I needed.* It's as if my mind was a shuffled pack of cards that has now been organised into suits, the hearts rising to the top of the pack, and spreading into my pounding chest like an army of soldiers on the verge of victory. *If we're lucky, everyone I've met so far might end up with a part in the play, too. Maybe I was wrong to judge them so harshly...the Troll Boys might not be so bad or dumb after all. They did chuck me in the pool, but they appear to have rescued me. So if they can help me, then, I suppose, I should help them...*

I blurt, 'Mousy...I mean Mia could play the Dormouse.' I cough to clear my croaky voice. 'She'd be perfect for the role...the Dormouse is always falling asleep.' I push my dripping hair away from my eyes.

Mia smiles at me. Her nose twitches before she asks, 'Does the Dormouse sleep throughout most of the play?'

'He does,' replies Toby. He turns to Mrs Royal. 'It's a great part for her, Miss, you've got to admit.'

Tobias nods rapidly. 'It's a brilliant part for her.'

Mia smiles. 'Perfect – I'm in.' Her grin breaks into a wide yawn.

Toby and Tobias are standing side-by-side, beaming like two boys who've cheated and won a game of cards when the odds were stacked against them. They both nod at one another before turning to me and signalling their approval with raised thumbs.

I feel a surge of strange and unexpected warmth, as if I've been accepted, as if I suddenly belong.

Tobias points at a name badge pinned to his blazer. Then, he points at his brother's badge. 'It's obvious what parts we should play, Miss. We're brothers, no one can tell us apart – that's why we wear these badges' – he pauses, waiting for Mrs Royal to respond – 'we could be–'

I interrupt, 'Tweedledum and Tweedledee!' They grin from ear to ear at my suggestion. I also think they'd make perfect mythological creatures – like a pair of trolls or one-eyed Cyclops in Sinbad, but I keep that to myself.

Mrs Royal places her hand on her hips. 'I'm hardly going to give them parts in the play after they've almost *drowned* you in the swimming pool on your first day!'

The brothers' faces drop. 'But...' they exclaim. Both boys' necks sink into their shoulders.

Mrs Royal wags her finger at them. 'What kind of example would I be making if–'

'The whole thing was my idea!' I blurt.

Mrs Royal turns to me. 'What was your idea?'

'Throwing me in the pool was my idea. I made them do it.'

Furrow lines appear on her brow. 'Why would you...?'

'I hit my head before I came into school today' – I touch the painful bump – 'on...on my mother's car door...I – I thought a dip in the water might help to liven me up a bit...I've not been feeling myself all morning.' I scramble to my feet. 'See, I'm feeling much better now.' I start to wobble. Within seconds, Tobias and Toby rush to my aid and wedge their bodies on either side of me, so that I'm propped up between them. 'Like the boys said, I've been trying to impress you with my acting skills, trying to re-enact parts from the two plays, so that you'd choose me to play one of the leading roles.'

The brothers smile at me, and then look at one another and nod.

Rebecca interjects, 'We've all been trying to help the new boy, Miss. Me and Mia helped him bathe the bump on his head with some water in the girls' toilets. Didn't we?' She looks at me, and I agree, forcing back a smile. 'But, unfortunately, it didn't help him much. But we tried, Miss.'

Mia adds, 'Then Tobias helped him get to your geography class on time while we stayed behind and mopped up the spilled water in the toilets.'

'That's why we were late for class, Miss,' insists Rebecca, twisting one of her ponytails round her finger. 'So, we shouldn't *really* have a detention later because we were only trying to help.'

Mrs Royal looks sceptically from one child to the next. 'But you implied' – she points at Toby – 'you threw him in the pool without knowing whether or not he could swim! He could've *drowned*!'

I interject, 'But they both saved me from drowning. And, I'm fine–'

Both boys nod enthusiastically.

'Oooooh! You boys, you're *impossible*! And the humidity in here is unbearable.' Mrs Royal pulls off her scarf and rubs the white rose pattern over her sweaty face so thoroughly that I fear the redness from her cheeks might bleed into the pattern and alter the colour of the roses. 'It's far too hot in here.' She waves the crumpled scarf in front of her face like a fan.

'Mrs Royal,' I blurt, 'you'd make a brilliant Queen of Hearts!'

She stops fanning herself. *'Me?'* She blushes, poised with her scarf dangling in her grip. Her cheeks glow even redder than before. 'Oh no, don't be silly...I – I couldn't possibly...do you *really* think so?'

Her eyes dart from one person to the next, eagerly waiting for their response.

'You *are* the best drama teacher *ever*, Miss,' exclaims Rebecca.

Mia adds, 'And you love the colour red.'

Mrs Royal looks down at her red dress. 'I do...' she says, deep in thought. 'I could...'

'No one could pull off the part like you, Miss,' insists Rebecca. Her fingers on both hands are crossed behind her back. 'I can hear you now, shouting: *"Off to the head!"'* She bites her bottom lip, and then mutters something about putting your hands on your head before she finally blurts, *'I mean, "Off with your head!"'*

Mrs Royal's face drops. 'But we *still* haven't resolved the problem I've had all along: *who would play Alice?'*

Tobias pats me on the back. My saturated clothing squelches against my body. 'I'm sure we'll find someone to play Alice, won't we, Gatter the Hatter.' He pats my back again.

'Gatter the Hatter?' says a girl, breathlessly. She giggles. 'That's a great nickname.'

I recognise the voice and whip round to face my sister.

'Hi, Thomas. You're okay then?'

'Yes, I'm fine, just a bit wet that's all.'

'I rushed here as quickly as I could.' She flattens down her dishevelled hair and readjusts her hair band. A few blades of dry grass fall from her locks. 'I'd fallen asleep on the field at break time when I heard some children hurrying past saying something about the new boy almost drowning in the pool. It took me longer than expected to get here because they'd blocked off one of the corridors to clear up some vomit.'

My eyes widen. I look at Tobias, staring at the floor, trying to hide his amusement. I smile nervously – *he obviously hasn't snitched on me about that yet either.*

My sister continues. 'I've been really worried about you– '

Tobias butts in, 'Aren't you going to introduce us, Gatter?'

'Oh...sorry...this is my sister Alice.'

He beams at her, wide-eyed.

Alice's eyes flicker over his badge. 'It's nice to meet you, Tobias Dunn.' She smiles.

Toby moves forward and extends his hand. 'I'm his brother, Toby Dunn.'

Alice reaches out with one hand to shake Toby's, and offers her other hand to Tobias to avoid hurting his feelings. 'You seem to have made some nice friends, Thomas. I haven't made *any* yet!'

My friends? A warm tingle spreads through my chest.

Tobias points at his brother. 'He might be playing the part of Tweedledee–'

Toby points to Tobias and adds, 'And he might be playing the part of Tweedledum in the school production of *Alice's Adventures in Wonderland.'*

Rebecca taps my shoulder. 'And your brother's probably landed the part of the Mad Hatter.' She continues, 'And I'm hoping to play the White Rabbit, or, maybe, the March Hare.' She nudges her sleepy-eyed friend. 'And I think Mia's going to be the Sleepy Dormouse.'

Mia regains her balance and speaks through a yawn, 'We just need to find someone to play Alice.'

My sister's eyes dart from one person to the next. 'I'm sure you'll find someone to play the part.'

'I'm Mrs Royal.' The teacher steps forward to shake Alice's hand. 'I've decided I'm going to play the Queen of Hearts.' She smiles, stepping back to look my sister up and down. 'Perfect...' Mrs Royal clears her throat. 'Tell me Alice Gatter, have you any acting experience? Your brother appears to be quite adept at method acting.'

Mrs Royal walks towards the pool exit, linking arms with Alice while explaining the importance of taking on the leading role in a play.

'Looks like we've found our Alice.' Toby chuckles.

Both looking very smug, Toby and Tobias grasp each other in a manly hug, bump tummies, jump and slap their hands together in a high-five.

Mrs Royal whips round in time to see both boys lose their balance on the slippery pool floor and fall on their bums. I burst out laughing as they sit there rubbing their bottoms and whimpering like wounded puppies.

The teacher's eyes narrow, but the hint of a smile betrays her otherwise angry face. *'Off with their heads!'* she shouts.

I swipe a finger across my neck and let my extended tongue droop from one side of my mouth before I fall to the floor, faking a dramatic death.

I hear my new friends sniggering as I lie on floor with one eye narrowly open, looking up at them. Their giggles turn into a chorus of painful cries. Then, bodies start falling to the floor all around me. I lift my head and look at my motionless mates' funny contorted faces.

Mrs Royal narrows her eyes and gives us a warm, but knowing smile. 'I'll see all of you on Thursday after school! Rehearsals are from three thirty until four thirty!'

Everyone sits up smiling and replies, 'Yes, Miss!'

'And don't be late!' With a glimmer of a smile and a satisfied nod, she exits the pool area through some double doors.

I grin like Lewis Carroll's Cheshire Cat and quote: *'"Almost everyone's mad here".'*

Tobias looks at his brother. 'Shall we chuck him back in the pool?'

Toby grins. 'Definitely.'

There's a playful scramble for my legs. But I'm on my feet within seconds and heading towards the exit. I quote: *'"And you may have noticed that I'm not all here myself!"'*

I look back at my crazy new friends slipping over the tiles behind me – laughing and cursing me at the same time – seconds before I scarper through the exit.

I was wrong – I think I'm going to like this school!

AUTHOR'S INSIGHT AND EDUCATIONAL NOTES

(Please read the following notes <u>after</u> reading the three stories)

Story 1: Blitz Spirit

I wrote this story in memory of my great grandparents who lived through the London Blitz in the Second World War. During an air raid, my mother, then a tiny baby, was rescued from their house by my great grandfather moments before the house was razed to the ground. If it were not for his bravery, I wouldn't be here today.

I decided to write this story from a **first person point of view** (limited point of view of the **protagonist**) in order for the reader to see the story unfold from the main character's perspective. My intention was to deceive you, leading you to believe that the protagonist was a young child and not a dog (Jack). If you read the story a second time, you might notice several hints in the text, which, if looked at more closely, would have been more obvious had you already known the protagonist's true identity from the onset: the dog has better hearing; he hates thunderstorms; he doesn't recognise the planes as anything more than large birds; he prefers the man in the butcher shop when Charlie prefers the lady in the sweet shop; the firemen ignore him initially, which they would not do if he were a child; he focuses heavily on Charlie's ball, which he knows he must not puncture like the last ball, while remaining focused on returning Charlie's ball to him and resuming their game of football as soon as possible.

I used the ball and the air within it to symbolise (**symbolism**) hope when Jack first finds it unscathed amidst the chaos and destruction. Jack gently holds the ball as if hanging on to the life of his friend. Later the air that remains in the ball also helps me to relay how the dog's fears are reduced when Charlie is found buried with some access to precious air: Jack doesn't want Charlie to be thrown away and never be seen again like the punctured ball, which had no remaining air.

I also used the bees in Charlie's grandfather's garden to **symbolise** how creatures normally prefer to live in harmony with their neighbours. However, if provoked, they, like ordinary people in the throes of war, will do everything to protect their homes and livelihoods. This section of the story also allowed me to give Jack a better understanding of the emergency services because he remembers the ambulance coming to help Charlie after he'd been stung by the bees.

The overall **theme** of this story was to highlight the importance of a bond between true friends, whether between two people or a person and a beloved animal. I also wanted to show how determination and strength of character during times when there appears to be no hope can pull you through even the most adverse situations.

I would like to thank all those unsung heroes, man or beast, for the bravery they have shown during natural and man-made disasters throughout history and today, most of whom none of us will never know.

Story 2: Mad Old Lady

At the beginning of this story, it is clear to the reader that Stacey (**protagonist**) believes the rumours about Mrs Craven when she argues with her mum and refuses to visit the old lady, totally misunderstanding her mother's good intentions.

I introduced the character Tom to highlight how Stacey starts off with conflicting views. She can see that Tom's lies will lead to no good, but this view is inconsistent with her open acceptance of the rumours spread about Mrs Craven, even when some of them are totally unbelievable: the old lady's apparent ability to look at people and turn them into stone.

The character Cameron allowed me to introduce Stacey's willingness to remain in denial about her feelings towards him – there's an obvious spark between them – and her feelings towards the rumours she has heard about Mrs Craven. When Stacey meets the old lady, she quickly discovers that the rumours are all exaggerated truths: Mrs Craven has two walking sticks instead of four legs; the windows of her house are blacked out to control light cycles for her plants and not for evil spells; the holes in her garden are from collecting soil, although Mrs Craven does express a wicked sense of humour when she admits that a few nosey children have inadvertently fallen into the large holes.

Mrs Craven's love for her plants is infectious, leaving Stacey questioning her animosity towards biology and her preconceptions about the old woman. Stacey dismisses several clues, which give the reader some doubts as to whether all is normal. The first hint in the text that Mrs Craven has passed away occurs when her grey cardigan is compared to wings and, shortly after, when her silhouette resembles an angel. Later, she mysteriously stops using her walking sticks, her appearance fades and her posture is more upright.

Mrs Craven uses her plants to educate Stacey in more than just horticulture when she points out that people are not the only creatures that can be fooled easily. Stacey discovers how altering light cycles can deceive plants, which she begins to compare to her own naive belief of the unsubstantiated rumours. She soon discovers that Mrs Craven is aware of all the ridiculous tales about her, leaving Stacey feeling ashamed that she was silly enough to believe them. Mrs Craven also uses the carnivorous plant Sarracenia Flava to show how the plant overcomes the usual restrictions of other plants by being different. This helps Stacey understand that she doesn't have to believe the vicious rumours just because everyone else does.

Near the end of the story, it's clear that Stacey regrets not visiting Mrs Craven when she was alive. As a consequence, her outlook on life, especially at school, and her relationship with her mother improves. Together they wait for the cutting taken from Mrs Craven's house to grow and bloom. When it does so, on the morning of Stacey's biology exam, the flower **symbolises** Stacey's blossoming future and doubles as a message from Mrs Craven – Rosa – wishing her good luck.

The overall **theme** of this story was to reiterate how important it is not to believe gossip and rumours without making your own unbiased observations first. People often grossly exaggerate and distort the truth into something that, for them, makes a story more exciting and engaging. Tales can often spread from one person to the next until the truth is twisted into untruth, causing irrevocable harm to the life of an innocent individual. I also wanted to highlight the contrast between the old lady's outward appearance and her inner beauty, and the dilapidated exterior of her home compared to the nurtured and beautiful flowers within, emphasising the old cliché *'never judge a book by its cover'*. A rose has an ugly, prickly stem, but when it blooms it's arguably the most beautiful of all flowers.

Story 3: A Curious First Day

This story was written as a tribute to the wonderful author Lewis Carroll, whose books – *Alice's Adventures in Wonderland* and *Through the Looking-Glass* – are possibly the funniest and maddest children's books ever written.

I chose a rather stuck-up boy – Thomas – to be my **protagonist** in order to show **character progression.** At the beginning of the story, Thomas has too many preconceptions about his new school and its pupils.

Unhappy about moving to a new area, he makes no effort to fit in or make friends. He refuses to refer to any of the children by their real names, giving them all nicknames – Tobias: Troll Boy, Rebecca: Floppy, Mia: Mousy – until the end of the story when he accepts them as friends and refers to them by their real names.

Every character was deliberately introduced with physical and personality traits similar to those in Lewis Carroll's books. Tobias and Toby Dunn are bumbling twins like Tweedledum and Tweedledee; Rebecca has ponytails like floppy rabbit ears and is constantly checking the time like the Rabbit; Mia has beady rodent eyes and is always falling asleep like the Sleepy Dormouse; Mrs Royal loves the colour red, she wears a scarf with rose print and likes to shout *'Hands on your head!'* or *'Off to the head!'* like the Queen of Hearts who bellows *'Off with their heads!'* If you were to read through the story again, you might notice earlier references to the books and the characters that you may have missed the first time. The following are two examples: Floppy – Rebecca – knocks into Thomas while checking her watch and stating that she is late at the beginning of the story, and slightly later when Thomas notices his locker key looking larger he questions whether it's because he suddenly feels ten times smaller.

I introduced the idea of the two productions – *Sinbad* and *Alice's Adventures in Wonderland* – to add confusion to the story. It also allowed Thomas's delirious mind to explore the two plays in which he is secretly wishing he'd play a leading role. In Thomas's mind, I was able to combine the productions and introduce some mythological creatures, treacherous seas, sailing and additional aspects from Lewis Carroll's books such as the walls and floors closing in on him – he wonders whether he is increasing in size or his surroundings are reducing.

The scene in the geography class was taken from personal experience. My geography teacher used to order anyone who uttered a word in her class to stand at the back of the classroom with their hands on their heads. As the class chatterbox, I was the first to suffer her wrath. However, I wasn't alone for long. Most of my classmates eventually joined me in a disorderly line of giggles and aching arms. Thank you, Mrs

Hallworth, for inspiring this scene. Although, I feel I should apologise to her for not including the stationary cupboard she used to lock us in – poor George spent almost every lesson in her cupboard! Perhaps, I thought it would make the scene feel...too unbelievable?

The **theme** of this story was to highlight how prejudice towards places and people you've never met can hold you back and dampen parts of your life that would otherwise be joyful. Be optimistic about the future, especially when you have no real reason to be pessimistic. Follow Thomas and steer the ship of life away from the jagged rocks. Life is what *you* make it!

GLOSSARY

Symbolism: The practice or art of using an object or a word to represent an abstract idea. When an author wants to suggest a certain mood or emotion, he can hint at it rather than blatantly saying it.

Theme: The story's message. It may be something that the reader thinks about after reading the story.

Protagonist: The main character in a story. Some books have more than one protagonist.

Character Progression: How a character changes throughout the story. This can have a positive or negative affect on the storyline, depending on the author's intended direction.

First Person Point of View: An author writes as if he is one of the characters, using pronouns such as: I, me, my, we, us, our.

Third Person Point of View: An author writes as an observer, as if he were watching a film, using pronouns such as: he, she, they, his, her.

Thank you...

I would like to thank everyone who supported and encouraged me throughout the writing of this book:

My family and friends: I always appreciate their readiness to help with proofreading and value their input at every stage. Most of the characters in my books are inspired by their warm and wonderful personalities. However, I'm sure they are able to recognise some of their grumpier and quirkier traits, which can prove equally useful.

My proofreader: A massive thank you to Andrew. His unwavering support never fails to boost my confidence. His expertise brings a succinct clarity to my work, which is absolutely essential to any good children's story. The time he dedicates to proofreading my work is always appreciated, probably more than he'll ever know.

The illustrator: My talented daughter Avril has, once again, used her unique style and combined the three very different stories in this book to produce a magnificent front cover. Unfazed by the task, she has created a mesmerising design that draws you in to the magical world of literature – the more I look at it, the more I want to see. Thank you, how can I ever express the full extent of my gratitude?

My readers: I'd like to thank you all from the bottom of my heart for your support. I really hope you enjoy these short stories as much as the Madder's World Trilogy. If you'd like to share your experience, contact me by email: scdann30@gmail.com. Alternatively, you can like my Madder's World Facebook page or log on to my website: www.scdannbooksblog.wordpress.com for all the latest information.

About the Author

Samantha lives in Norfolk with her husband, four children, her dog, chickens and two fish. She plays the piano, enjoys long walks with her dog, loves cycling and is an avid reader.

Since the publication of her **Madder's World** books, Samantha has been working hard to bring you this, her first short story book. All four books are available through Amazon in paperback and Kindle format.

Once again, Samantha has collaborated with her daughter (Avril) who also designed this book's intricate and vibrant front cover.

Samantha hopes her short stories will be received as warmly as her previous books, allowing her to continue writing for many years to come...